Love Me...Please

International Award-Winning Author
Toneal M. Jackson

www.WeAreAPS.com

Monique

..."Love me, please. Amen."

Growing up, Monique had always known there was something different about her. She didn't look like the rest of her family, and she always seemed to march to the beat of her own drummer. When looking at family pictures, she tormented herself struggling to find any resemblance.

She loved her parents, and appreciated every effort provided to take care of her. However, something was missing, and she knew it was time to find out what. Tired of the internal conflict, she decided that now was the time to ask her parents that burning question, "Am I adopted"? At this point, she was 18, a legal adult, so what harm could it do to know the truth? One fateful Friday night, Monique mustered the courage to confront her parents.

"Mom, Dad, I have something I want to ask you. It's been on my mind for some time now, and well, I'm kinda unsure of how to ask" she rambled while playing with her fingers.

"Just ask already, Monique" her Dad interrupted. "You know how much I hate it when you drag stuff out".

"Am I adopted?" Monique blurted out, eyes closed.

Her mother just looked in disbelief; her father was awe-stricken.

"Monique, why would you ask such a thing? Don't you know how much your father and I love you?" her mother defensively retorted.

"Mom, I wasn't trying to make you feel bad, or question you and Dad's love, it's just something I wanted to know" Monique said while dropping her head.

Her mother glanced at Monique, then at her husband. She took a deep breath and said, "Bill, I think we ought to tell her".

"Tell me what?" Monique asked.

"Well, I don't quite know where to begin".

"At the beginning" Monique mumbled.

"Well, Monique, I guess you could say that you are adopted. I mean, I did give birth to you, but you dad adopted you when you were 10 months old. He and I thought that doing it this way would be better…"

"Better than what?" Monique interrupted ecstatically.

"Better than knowing the truth" her mother continued.

"And what would that be?"

Monique asked.

"Well, the fact of the matter is that your biological father and I were friends, and well one night, things went a bit further than either of us meant them to go, and well, nine months later, you were born".

"And none of this time you thought I would've wanted to know? That I might want to actually have a relationship with my *real* father"?

"Wait a minute, Monique" her Dad said while rising.

"What do you mean – real father? I have been a real father to you. Have you ever wanted for anything"?

"Dad, I'm sorry. I didn't mean it that way. It's just, wow…all of this is sort of overwhelming to digest".

"And that's why we didn't want to tell you" her mother chimed in. "We knew it would be too much to handle".

"Well, does my biological father know that I exist, or was I kept secret from him too"?

"He knows" her mother whispered.

"He knows?" Monique repeated in disbelief.

Then disbelief transitioned to anger.

"He knows! He knows!

Well, where is he if he knows? Where has he been for the past 18 years if he knows? He knows I'm alive? He knows I'm his kid? So, all of this time *everyone* has known, but me"?

Her mother extended her hand to try to console her daughter, but she could tell it was too late. Monique was in a frenzy, so now the only comfort she could offer her daughter was the truth.

"Monique, it wasn't a proud moment for me. I was ashamed of what I'd done, and I knew that he wasn't going to take care of you. But I thought the least I could do was to let him know. So I told him that I was pregnant and that he was the father.

He didn't make me feel bad, he just solemnly told me that it was up to me if I wanted to go through with the pregnancy. I told him of course, because I didn't believe in abortion.

He told me that he wasn't willing to give up his career to settle down and raise a family. I told him that it was his choice. I never forbade him not to see you, he just never made the time.

Then Bill and I met; we fell in love and decided to get married. So we thought it was better that he adopt you – I mean, you were only a few months old. We figured that beyond biology, what was important was to have two parents who were present to love you consistently. If we were wrong for that, then we're sorry."

"So, he just…he never wanted me" Monique managed to utter, holding back her tears.

"It wasn't like that, sweetheart" her mother responded. "He knew that I'd gotten married, and that Bill was a good person, and well, he just thought it would be confusing for you – him popping in and out of your life all the time. This was his way of providing you with a sense of stability".

"So what about now? I'm 18, no longer a child…what's his

excuse now? Why hasn't he picked up a phone or sent me a text? He hasn't even friended me on Facebook! If he wanted to be part of my life, he could've been. There are no excuses. So like I said, he just never wanted me" sobbed Monique.

Syrae

..."Love me, please. Amen."

"Another day, another dollar" said Syrae as she put on her shirt. She looked at her bed in disgust, as he rolled over. What was his name again?

She couldn't recall. He was just one of many. Not a name, not a face, not even a memory. Just something she did to make it through the day. The only way she knew to earn some real money.

"When did it come to this?" she wondered as she brushed her teeth. It was while washing her face that she realized she had no idea who it was she was looking at in the mirror.

It seemed like just yesterday...

"Syrae, Syrae, come here. I've got something I want you to see" her mother beckoned anxiously.

"What is it, Mom? I'm trying to finish my homework" Syrae responded.

"You can finish that later. You *have* to see this" her mother exclaimed.

Syrae put her pencil down and ran up the stairs.

"Yeah, Mom, what is it?"

"Isn't this the most beautiful dress you've ever seen?" her mom asked.

Syrae looked at the dress in amazement. She had to admit it was beautiful; it had the right amount of sparkle, but most importantly, it was purple – her favorite color.

"What is this, Mom? Who is it for?" she asked, secretly hoping it was for her.

"Well" her mother began. "I know your Spring Dance is approaching, and I know that you don't have anything to wear, so..."

"Mom, you're the best!" Syrae shouted as she embraced her mother. "I didn't think you would...I mean, it's perfect –THANK YOU!"

"Don't thank me, thank your father. He was adamant about getting you this dress. He said he knew it would look good on you and fit you well. I just picked it up" her mother explained.

"So *he* picked this out? And you bought it? I can't believe this" said Syrae as she threw the dress on the floor and slammed out of the room.

In disbelief herself, Syrae's mother hung her head. "I can't believe this child. I go out of my way to do something nice. Work all of this overtime, just so I can afford the dress...and she throws it on the floor? Wait until her father gets home. He's going to have to deal with this".

Shortly after, Syrae's father came home.

"Percy" Syrae's mom called. "Is that you"?

"Yeah, hon" he replied.

"Can you come upstairs for a moment? I need to talk to you".

"I'm on my way".

As he approached the doorway, he noticed the purple dress on the floor. He picked it up and inquired, "What is this about? Don't tell me she didn't like it".

"I don't know what's going on" her mother remarked. "I thought she'd love it, you know, appreciate that this is the reason I've been working so much lately. I would do anything in the world for Syrae, but sometimes..."

"Don't worry, dear" Percy assured his wife, "I'll take care of it".

Syrae lie idle on the bed. Then she began crying uncontrollably.

"It's all my fault" she whispered. "If it wasn't for me wanting that stupid dress, Mom would've been here. She would've known. That's why he said that she'd be mad at me. I can't believe it...it's all my fault" she repeated. She began to cry hysterically into her pillow when she heard a knock on her door.

"Who is it?" she asked, wiping the tears from her

eyes.

Without a reply, her dad walked through the door.

"Syrae, I want to talk to you" he said as he sat on the bed next to his daughter. "What would make you throw the dress that your mother worked so hard to buy for you, on the floor? Do you know how that made her feel"?

"I wasn't trying to hurt Mom" she sarcastically replied.

"I was just mad because she said YOU picked it. That you told her it would look good on me and fit me well" she continued while moving toward her dresser.

"Oh, so you didn't want to look good for your Daddy?" Percy asked while walking toward her.

"Of course, I know what looks good on you. I know you – inside and out – don't you ever forget that".

How could she forget? Every night for the last two months she received unwelcomed visits, unwanted touches. True, she'd always dreamt of her first time. But never in a million years did she think it would be with her own father.

"Syrae".

Syrae shook her head as she was brought back to reality. She turned from the bathroom mirror to focus her attention on, Wait, what was his name again?

Aniyah

..."Love me, please. Amen."

The youngest of four, Aniyah had always known about responsibility. Her mom, a single parent, had no choice but to show her girls at an early age about accountability. They were a close-knit family that depended on one another to survive.

Although all of the girls were assigned chores, Aniyah took pride in completing her tasks; she possessed a deep desire to please her mother. Whenever her sisters failed to do their chores, it was Aniyah to the rescue.

She'd done everything by the book – graduated from high school, check. Unlike her sister Alicia who dropped out her junior year, Aniyah knew it was important to finish school. It had broken her mother's heart when her sister dropped out, and Aniyah wasn't about to make the same mistake.

Received a college degree, check. She was always told about the opportunities associated with being a college graduate. All the ways it could elevate your career in the work force.

When her sister Alexis informed her mother that college was not in her future - that she'd prefer to pursue a singing career, Aniyah's mom was in total disbelief. Aniyah knew there was no way she would add to that grief for their mother.

Got married before having children, check. Her mother shared with Aniyah the difficulties she had being a single parent, and how having someone to help would prevent so much of the struggle – words which her sister Ashley never heeded. At this point, Ashley had two children by two different guys, and wasn't looking to settle down any time soon. Although Aniyah was young when she married (straight out of college), she knew it was a decision that made her mother proud.

As Aniyah reflected on her life, she realized that much of it was lived for her mother's approval, decisions she'd now began to question.

"Sorry for your loss"

words she struggled to process. What does that even mean? Sorry for your loss? It just sounds like an empty phrase people use because they have nothing else to say.

"Sorry for your loss" – it just wouldn't stop! People walking around, grabbing her hand, some even trying to embrace her.

Everyone's face was a blur. In fact, this entire day was beyond comprehension. What had happened? What had gone on? She repeatedly asked herself those questions.

Technically, she understood WHAT happened, but it didn't matter though. She felt totally helpless. There was nothing she could do to alter the outcome.

Although her mother always equipped her with knowledge necessary to prevent making common mistakes, no amount of words, no amount of deeds, no amount of anything would change this inevitable disaster.

"Mom, you never told me how to handle *this* experience" she sadly whispered, staring at her mother's casket.

Mentally, she knew what to do. She knew how to contact the funeral home; she could write the obituary; and calling everyone about the arrangements was no problem. But emotionally, she was a wreck!

She wasn't prepared to handle something of this magnitude. It hadn't even been a year since she married, and just recently learned she was pregnant, and now this? To make matters worse, it had been months since she'd spoken to her sisters.

Sure they were at her wedding because her mother threatened them of what would happen if they didn't show. But only her mother knew of her pregnancy. She hadn't had the opportunity to tell anyone else; due to her mother's illness, she felt it paled in comparison. Her primary focus was on doing whatever was necessary to get her mother better.

She quit her job, became her mother's caregiver, even her faith in God increased. Everyone always complimented her on the level of strength she demonstrated throughout the entire ordeal.

What they didn't know was that she totally depended on her mother. Even through the sickness, Aniyah's expectation was that her mother would pull through. She needed her mother to make it, but she didn't. Her mother was a strong woman, but unfortunately, Cancer was stronger.

Aniyah

Now with her mother gone, Aniyah was going to have to face reality on her own. Without her mother's influence, she was lost. All she had left were her sisters. And at this point, was reconciliation even possible?

Barbara

… "Love me, please. Amen."

"You may now kiss the bride", six words that it seemed Barbara had waited her entire life to hear. Who would've thought that 20 years had passed since they'd been uttered?

Now, Barbara felt like an old maid. She'd given birth to three beautiful children, two of which had already moved, and the last one was a senior in high school. Barbara had dedicated her life to taking care of her husband and her children, ensuring that every need was met, never taking any time for herself. After 20 years, she'd lost her identity – who was she? What did she like to do?

Everything she had become was in direct relation to her children or her husband. She was no longer Barbara; she was either Cheryl's, Charlie's or Cherie's mother, or Charles' wife. Her most common reference was Mrs. Tate; it tended to be all-encompassing.

With her children grown, she knew that she would now be forced to deal with her marriage. For the past decade, it had been in shambles, but with the children serving as distractions, she could focus her attention on the positivity that came with being a mother.

She loved her husband, but it had been a long time since things had been right between them. She'd lost respect for him long ago due to his constant degradation. It seemed he got a thrill out of criticizing her. He couldn't even do it behind closed doors – no, he had to wait until there was a crowd.

Oh, the shame she felt.

But he didn't care. The more she told him how embarrassed and hurt she was by his remarks, the more he made them. He felt justified in mistreating his wife. And she understood the reasoning.

Yes, she had an affair, but that had been almost 10 years ago. He meant that he wasn't going to let her live it down.

She understood it was wrong, but she was tired of trying to fix her marriage by herself. Having empty conversations. Begging her husband to spend time with her.

She'd done everything she knew to do to try to communicate, but nothing helped. In fact, it seemed that "talking" just pushed them farther apart. He would become irritated, she more frustrated. Why was she wasting her breath trying to get him to understand her perspective?

She stopped talking, stopped trying. She lived her life in auto-pilot mode, just existing. Spoke only when spoken to. Helped her kids whenever requested. She was no longer Barbara, she was just a shell – purposed only to serve others. She had slipped into a depression, not knowing how to come out – not caring IF she came out.

Then one day while in the checkout line at the grocery store, the cashier asked her a question.

"Who made you mad?" he

snickered.

"I'm sorry, what?" Barbara replied. She was so busy daydreaming that she hadn't heard him.

"I said, why are you looking so angry? You're way too pretty to have that expression on your face" he continued.

Without knowing it, Barbara smirked.

"Oh, so you can smile" joked the cashier.

Barbara finished putting her groceries on the conveyor belt and asked, "How much do I owe you?"

She paid her tab and as she was

walking away she turned and said, "Have a good day".

The cashier retorted, "I will, and you do the same".

While loading the car, Barbara reflected on the interaction that just occurred. Had he called her pretty? She couldn't even remember the last time she'd allowed herself to release a smile.

She was grateful for that cashier. For a brief moment, she felt good about herself again. She then realized that she hadn't even asked his name.

Monique

Weeks had passed since Monique learned the devastating news regarding her biological father. No matter how hard she tried not to think about him, that's all her mind focused on.

What did he look like now? Did she resemble him? Did she have any brothers or sisters? What were her family members like on her father's side? All of these questions ran through her mind repeatedly.

She wanted to ask her mother, but she didn't want to torment her. Her mother was already heartbroken when she had to tell Monique the truth, and she didn't want to worsen the situation. However, the fact was that Monique just had to know – her curiosity was getting the best of her.

Monique was constantly battling with her emotions. One moment she felt total anxiety; not knowing the details of her family history was overwhelming. But on the other hand, she was fearful.

What happened if she reached out to her father, but he didn't bother to reciprocate her efforts? After all, this was the same man that had known for 18 years that she'd existed, and hadn't taken the time to mail a letter or even pick up a phone. Why should she think things would be different now…or that he'd be different? What she'd learned was only news for her — he'd already known!

So after deliberating heavily and weighing her options, Monique decided that she did want to make contact with her father. She felt he owed her an explanation. She understood her mother's perspective; many of Monique's friends were teenage mothers raising their children without help, so she admired her mom for making such a difficult decision.

The more she thought about it, it couldn't have been

easy for her mother to raise her, looking at her everyday – especially if she resembled her father. That had to serve as a constant reminder of a night that her mother wanted so much to forget. But at least her mother stuck it out.

And Bill, well her dad for intents and purposes, came into a ready-made family and really stepped up to the plate. How many men volunteer to take care of somebody else's child? Not many; he had done something that her own father hadn't been man enough to do. For that, she would always be eternally grateful and consider Bill as her dad.

However, she still longed for

the truth – from the mouth of her father. She wanted to hear what he could possibly say to justify his absence for 18 years. Now, she simply had to decide *how* to reach out to him.

Should she call him? After the conversation she'd had with her parents, her mother provided her with the latest phone number she had, as well as a picture she dug up from an old photo album. Monique decided against calling him since she'd never heard his voice. She couldn't be certain that whomever answered the phone would be her father.

And even if it was, how do you start *that* conversation, "Hi,

I'm your daughter Monique that you've avoided for the past 18 years, how are you?" Monique thought it better to eliminate the sarcasm if she wanted to gain any ground with him.

Then she thought about writing a letter; however this method was problematic for two reasons. First and foremost, she didn't know where he lived, so even if the letter was written, it would go undelivered. Second, Monique felt she could encounter similar issues as she would've with a phone call.

Although she had no problems expressing herself, since she didn't know him, a letter may come across as impersonal, or perhaps crude. She wanted her first impression to be memorable, but positive.

Because he didn't know her or her intentions, he might take what she had to say offensively; even worse, he might not respond at all. That was the last thing Monique desired. If she was going to make contact, it was going to have to be more personable.

She concluded that she would employ the services of Facebook to make this connection. The plan was actually perfect the more she thought about it. If she friended him, he'd have the opportunity to see who she was, and if his information wasn't private, she could collect some facts about him. At the very least she could determine if he lived in the same city or state.

As luck would have it, his information was public…and what was this? He too resided in Chicago! Wow, maybe this truly was meant to be. Monique had done her part; she clicked "Add Friend". Now, all she could do was wait for him to respond to her request.

Syrae

Every day for the past few weeks it seemed as though something happened to Syrae to trigger her past. She'd worked so hard to forget the dreadful thing. I mean it had been years since she was molested by her father. Years since he raped her. But for whatever reason, every time she laid down with a different guy, childhood memories would come rushing back.

She had made peace with what had become her life. Was she pleased with what had become her existence?

Absolutely not. But after such a traumatic upbringing, it was almost impossible to identify a "right" decision.

She thought it was the right decision to tell her father to leave her alone; to stop coming in her room; to stop touching her. But what resulted from those efforts? In addition to getting raped, she got beaten.

And every time, he'd threaten her life if she told anyone – especially her mother. So for months she'd walk around with hidden bruises, and hollow on the inside – all for making what she thought was the right decision.

She thought it the right decision to finally tell her mother the hell that had become her life. The agony that she experienced on a daily basis. So one day she mustered the courage, while HE was gone, to talk to her mom.

"Mom, I need to talk to you. Are you busy?"

"Syrae, you know I'm never too busy for you. Come in and sit down. What's going on?"

"Well, Mom" Syrae began, "I don't know how to tell you. I've really been struggling to find the right words to say, but there are none".

"Syrae, what's wrong? Talk to me. You know you can tell me anything".

"I hope so" she muttered under her breath. "Well, um, for the past few months, I've been raped repeatedly – and beaten. I don't even know how to hide the bruises anymore" Syrae just barely audible.

"Wait, what? Syrae, why are you just now telling me? Oh, my God - are you okay? Of course you're not okay...what am I saying? Baby, all this time you've been walking around hurting. I mean, I noticed you'd become a bit reclusive, but I thought it was just a phase.

When I discussed it with your father, he said you'd just been having some tough times, but that you would be okay. That the best thing to do would be to leave you alone and give you time to work it out on your own".

"And you believed him" Syrae interrupted.

"Yes. Why wouldn't I? He's your father. I know with me working so much lately, you two have become a lot closer."

"Closer than you think" whispered Syrae. "What makes you think that we're so close?" she asked in a tone loud enough for her mother to hear.

"Because he's always talking about you, Syrae. Always saying how much he loves you. How proud he is of you. How beautiful you are. How you're growing into a fine young lady".

Syrae couldn't believe what she was hearing. This piece of crap actually had the nerve to be discussing her with her mother? He truly was unconscionable. At this point, she was wondering just how much he'd told her.

"So he told you all of that, huh? Did he tell you anything else?"

"Like what, Syrae?" her mother inquired.

"Like he's the reason I've been so, what was the word you used – reclusive? I've been wearing black for the last I don't know how long, trying to be invisible; praying that he would leave me alone. But wearing black can only cover up so much for so long".

"Syrae, what are you saying?" her mom asked trying to make sense of her daughter's news.

"Mom, don't you get it? *He's* the reason I wear black. I'm depressed because of him, Mom. Because of what he's been doing to me."

"Like what, Syrae? What are you trying to say?" Her

mom wanted to know.

Syrae didn't know how to make it any more plain. She was hoping that her mother could put two and two together, but obviously not. So she knew she was just going to have to say the words.

"For the past few months, he's been beating me" Syrae finally managed to force out. She figured that since her mom was having such a difficult time comprehending, it might be best to start with the "good" news first.

"Why would he beat you, Syrae? Your father loves you" her mother insisted.

"Please, don't call him my father" Syrae retorted. "To answer your question, he beat me because he wanted to make sure I never told you".

"Told me what?" her mother asked cutting her off.

"That he's been raping me, Mom" Syrae blurted out no longer able to hold back the tears. "He's been raping me – repeatedly. And I have to see his face everyday.

I can't get away from him. No matter how early I try to leave for school; no matter how late I come back home.

There is no escape. My

life has been torture, Mom –
excruciating torment that
I've had to deal with by
myself. It's like I've been
living in silence, so afraid to
say anything."

"Well, if that's the case
Syrae, if your father has
been touching you like you
say, why now all of a sudden,
have you gotten this
newfound courage to speak
up?"

"What?" Syrae couldn't
believe her ears. "What do
you mean IF that's the case?
IF he's been touching me?
Newfound courage?"

Syrae didn't know where
to begin. Was her mother

actually questioning her story? Was she accusing her of lying? She knew she had to set the record straight.

"Trust me Mom, it IS the case – it has been happening. Why would I make up something like this? And no, I didn't say *touching*, I said *raping*! For the past five months your husband has been raping me.

Almost every night for five months, I've had to deal with that, Mom. Do you know how it's made me feel? Having to go through this alone? I mean, who could I tell?

What family do we have?

Both you and he are only children. And, if I told the people at school, they'd probably have to investigate."

"So if all of this is true, Syrae, why didn't you tell them – let them investigate?"

"Because I didn't want to hurt you, Mom" Syrae uttered in disbelief. "As much as I hate him, I love you more, and I didn't want anyone to take me away from you. So I just dealt with it."

"And now?" her mom asked.

"And now, what?" Syrae retorted not knowing where her mother was going with her line of questioning.

"I'm asking again, why have you waited until now to tell me, Syrae? You've kept it to yourself all this time; why are you choosing this moment to tell me?"

"Are you serious?" was all Syrae could manage to say.

Was she for real? Well, there goes any support system she might need. Syrae knew she was going to have to do this on her own.

She simply replied, "Because now, I'm pregnant".

Aniyah

It had been months since her mother's funeral, and Aniyah was still struggling to cope. The first weeks or so after her mom died, Aniyah was depressed. Although she'd seen her sisters, they just barely spoke; they didn't even come to the repast Aniyah had at her house.

What made matters worse was that she had to suffer through this alone. She didn't want to tell her husband, because he'd only tell her that she couldn't allow herself to become stressed out over things she couldn't change. It wasn't that he was wrong, but the fact was they were still her sisters, and it was really starting to bother her that they were not on speaking terms.

Usually, she'd ask her mom for advice on how to handle such a situation. In fact, it wasn't long after her death that Aniyah actually picked up the phone to call her mother. It wasn't until she heard the operator say, "I'm sorry, the number you have dialed has been disconnected" that Aniyah was reminded of the harsh reality that had become her life.

Now, she had to figure this out on her own. How was she going to get her sisters to speak to her again…especially when she wasn't sure what caused them to stop in the first place. Aniyah began to assess the situation to see if she could determine why her sisters were so disgruntled toward her.

She reflected on conversations she'd had with her mother…

"Mom, I don't get it" Aniyah began. "Why does it seem like my sisters hate me all of a sudden? They don't call me like they used to – much less stop by to say hello".

In spite of her illness, her mother always managed to provide Aniyah with words of wisdom.

"Give them some time, Aniyah. You have to understand that everyone has their own way of dealing with things. You've done everything right with your life, and made all the proper choices – graduated from high school; got your college degree; and got married…all before having a child.

And before I got sick and you decided to quit, you were very successful on your job. So when your sisters see that, it causes a little bitterness.

Because you're the youngest, they were probably expecting to be an example for you, but instead they've always had to look to you for help.

That can be a pretty humbling experience because it forces you to recognize the consequences you've had to face due to bad decisions; trust me, I've been there and done that.

That's why I always tried my best to prepare you girls for the world ahead. Unfortunately, you were the only one who listened. But, just give them time…they'll come around. Remember, your sisters love you, and although you all are going through a rough patch now – and it may not seem like it – this too shall pass.

"This too shall pass" Aniyah mouthed the words with her eyes closed. It seemed that was her mother's favorite phrase; her way of saying that no matter how bad a situation might be – it wouldn't last forever. And, it never did. Her mother had a habit of being right. Now, Aniyah was hoping that this time wouldn't be any different.

Although Aniyah didn't dispute her mother's words, she didn't understand why they would be true. Why should the decisions she made cause bitterness for her sisters? They were all equally intelligent, and equipped to handle any situation; they learned that from their mother.

Even though Alicia dropped out of high school, she ended up going back a few years later and receiving her GED. She even went to vocational school, and picked up a trade – a talent that she still employs.

After Alexis graduated from high school, it wasn't long before she was singing with a group. Heck, she'd even become a local celebrity. If only their lead singer wouldn't have been killed. Who knows where singing could've taken her? But after seeing her best friend gunned down, Alexis no longer had the desire to stick with it.

And Ashley? Well, Ashley always did manage to march to the beat of her own drummer, a trait that Aniyah strongly admired. True, over the years Aniyah had to take in her sister and her children a couple of times, but it was never for extended periods.

Ashley was so resilient – probably the most of the all four girls. She never allowed any situation to get the best of her. She'd been in some tough relationships and she never complained. She'd tell Aniyah, "I made this bed, now I have to lie in it".

Aniyah never understood her sister's strength. Ashley had finally come to the conclusion that she didn't need a man to take care of her. She decided she had all the skills necessary to provide for herself and her children.

She began a career in healthcare; although the hours were sometimes long and the time away from her children unbearable, Ashley had truly become independent. Most importantly, she was now proud of the example she had become for her children.

The only thing Aniyah could deduce was that she'd made better consecutive choices. Because the truth was, she admired the courage of all of her sisters. They were all brave enough to step out on their own to pursue their respective paths without fear. They'd learned much earlier what Aniyah was just finding out — it's not always a good decision to live your life for someone else.

That said, she had to figure out what to do to reestablish the lines of communication with her sisters. She could reflect all day on would've, could've, should've, but that wasn't going to resolve the issue at hand.

She was now seven months pregnant and her sisters still didn't know. Just then, it hit her: "I'll have a baby shower and invite them. All they can do is say no". Smiling, Aniyah immediately began planning the event she hoped would reunite her and her sisters.

Barbara

Barbara and Charles were preparing to go to marriage counseling; after all, it was Tuesday. Every Tuesday, for the past eight years they went, like clockwork.

"You just about ready, Barbara?" Charles asked.

"Yeah, just about" Barbara replied.

She didn't understand why, after eight years, they were still attending counseling sessions. I mean, what more could be said that hadn't been expressed one hundred times over? However, she was committed to making her marriage work; she had no problem taking accountability for her actions.

But at what point was Charles going to acknowledge that how he treated her contributed to her infidelity? A question that even Dr. Adams had posed numerous times.

"Alright, I'm ready to go" stated Barbara.

The two hopped in the car for what was usually a two hour drive. Initially, Barbara would try to make small talk. But after awhile, she found that it was just easier to ride in silence, as questions typically provoked argument.

The topic never mattered; she could ask Charles something as simple as what he wanted her to pick up from the grocery store, and that would be trouble. His response, "I don't know why you still even going to the grocery store. As I recall, last time you went, you brought home more than groceries".

Remembering Dr. Adams' words, she'd just take a deep breath and calmly reply, "Charles, that was almost ten years ago. I just went to the store Saturday and I believe I was alone when I came home".

"Yeah, maybe THIS time, but that wasn't always the case, now was it?" he'd sarcastically retort.

"It wasn't just this time; and again it has been the case for over eight years now. But if it's too painful for you, the thought of my going to the grocery store, I've told you before that you're welcome to do the shopping" Barbara would shoot back.

"Did I ask to do the shopping?" he'd ask nastily.

"No, but if every time I talk about the grocery store you feel the need to bring up my affair, then I would prefer you be the one to make the trip. I just want some resolve with this situation" Barbara would mutter.

So after a few months of riding

with unproductive conversation, she decided not to talk, but to listen to the radio. Sure enough, every song that played had something to do with cheating; that would start similar arguments. So Barbara decided it best to just ride in silence – what had now become a 7-year ritual.

When they finally arrived to Dr. Adams' home, they rang the bell and Dr. Adams greeted them and led them to the family room, which he used for counseling sessions.

"So, where shall we begin tonight?" Dr. Adams questioned.

"Well, doc" Charles began, "I'm still experiencing issues coping with Barbara's infidelity. I know it was a long time ago, but I'm still having nightmares and waking in cold sweats. I'm trying to move past it as you've suggested, but I'm stuck. I want to forgive her, but every time I close my eyes, all I can see is her in the arms of another man — well, shall I say boy…grocery boy, at that".

What was this? After eight years, had Dr. Adams made a new discovery?

"Charles, in all this time, you've never mentioned that you were bothered by the age difference. Let's explore that".

"What's to explore" Charles

wondered.

"Barbara, I know we've gone over this countless times, but would you mind recounting the details of your indiscretion?" Dr. Adams requested.

Although Barbara thought it was pointless, she complied.

"Well, like I've told you before, for me, it initially started with a flirtatious interaction. He (for Charles' sake was the agreed upon reference name) made me feel special the first time I met him. I know Charles believes it was more, but it wasn't; it honestly did start out that innocently.

Smiling again after such a

long time made me want to find out more about him. So I returned to the grocery store simply wanting to thank him for helping me to smile again. Except when I returned, he was nowhere to be found. So I just let it go – you know, said never mind. I left the grocery store to get something to eat at a nearby restaurant, and as it happened, he was there.

I approached him, and thanked him for his comments. He asked me to join him at his table, so I did. Next thing I knew, we'd been there for hours – just talking. It was so comforting to have someone appreciate me for me as a person – not what I was doing for them, and not being condescending all the time – something I had become accustomed to with Charles.

He sparked something in me that I'd forgotten about…me! I forgot that I could be funny; forgot that I possessed the ability to make people laugh. I'd become so serious, just taking care of others all the time. I no longer had friends, so once I acquired one, I didn't want to let him go."

"So for you, it had nothing to do with age" Dr. Adams interjected.

"Absolutely not. In fact, I think he was only maybe six years younger; so it's not like he needed a chaperone to be with me. If you ask me, Charles is just using the 'age difference' as a smoke screen".

What do you mean?" asked Dr. Adams.

"The bottom line is that as long as we can focus on what I did wrong, we will never focus on Charles' shortcomings or the things that he can do to become a better husband. And until we conquer those issues, our marriage will never improve.

Monique

After waiting what seemed like an eternity, Monique finally received a response. To her surprise, not only had her father accepted her friend request, but he had also sent her a message.

"Monique, I am so delighted to hear from you. I hope that all is well with you. I know that you probably have a lot of questions for me – questions that I will gladly address. If you're not busy this Friday, I'd love to meet you and have this conversation over dinner. Let me know if you're available. Your father, Jeff."

Wow, Monique could hardly believe her eyes. Was this actually happening? Was she actually being presented with the opportunity to meet her father? Friday was only three days away! Monique quickly replied to the message, "I'd love to. Please send me the details."

She just sat in the chair in total disbelief. She wondered if it would have been this easy had she known earlier. How much of a relationship would she have had with her father had she discovered the truth years before?

Monique decided it was senseless to torture herself,

because she would never know what could've been. Thinking about it repeatedly wouldn't change the past; however, focusing on the present could definitely alter the future. She was finally going to meet her father! It was in the midst of her excitement that she realized she had yet to tell her parents about the interaction. How would this news affect them?

Monique looked out of the window and noticed her parents' cars in the driveway. Since they were both home, why not tell them now? All of a sudden, she began sweating, and she could feel a lump in her throat.

Why was she so nervous? It's not like this was a surprise. Her parents knew her well enough to know that she wouldn't just leave the situation alone. So where was all of this anxiety coming from? If she was just providing them an update, why was she feeling so bad? What did she have to feel guilty about? It's not like *she* was hiding the truth from *them*. So, what was the problem?

"I don't want to hurt them" Monique mumbled. "What if, when I tell them, they feel betrayed? I don't want this to be like a slap in the face".

Monique was trying to rationalize her feelings about the extenuating circumstances. "This is a mess" she stammered. "No matter what I do, it's a chance that I will hurt them. If I tell them, they might get offended. If I don't, it's like I've got something to hide. I just don't know what to do".

As her mind continued to wander, there was a knock on the door.

"Who is it?" called Monique.

"It's Mom, can I come in?"

"Sure" Monique said as she opened the door.

"Hey, Sweetie. What'cha been up to?"

Monique could look at her mother and tell that there was something on her mind.

"Nothing much, Mom. What's up?"

"Well, I know that things have been a little awkward for all of us lately. I know it hasn't been easy for you to process everything. I'm sure you still have some confusion – some inner conflict left unresolved, and I want you to know that your father and I, I mean, Bill and I – I mean, well now I don't know what I mean because I don't know how you see things. I guess what I want to know is, has learning the truth changed your feelings about me and your dad?"

Monique was shocked. Never before could she

remember her mother in such a state of uncertainty. Her mother was always so poised and confident; but now, it seemed she was moments away from a breakdown. What had she done to her mother? Finding out she was adopted was like opening Pandora's Box.

"Monique, did you hear me?" her mother repeated.

Monique had become so lost in her own thoughts that she had totally tuned out her mother.

"Sure, Mom" Monique replied.

"So you want to?" her mom asked.

"Want to what?" she inquired totally confused.

"Go to the movie – Monique, what is going on with you? Aren't you listening?"

"Of course, I'm listening" she lied. "And of course I want to go".

"Great" her mother exclaimed. "Your dad is going to be so pleased. The movie comes out Friday, so we can go once your dad gets back from work. We should be able to make the 7 o'clock show. In fact, we'll make a night of it; after the movie, we can go grab a bite to eat. Monique, I really believe that this is just what we need to get us back on track."

Her mother hugged her tight, kissed her on the forehead and vanished.

What in the world just happened? Monique felt as though she'd been caught in a whirlwind. Had she just agreed to plans with parents? Did her mother say "Friday"? As in *THIS* Friday? As in the same Friday that she'd arranged to meet for dinner with her father, Friday?

As if things weren't already complicated enough, now she'd double-booked with all of her parents. Her mother was so happy, there was no way she could tell her that she'd already made plans. And after that "this is just what we need to get back on track" line – forget about it.

But Monique didn't want to cancel her plans with her biological father either. It had taken 18 years to arrange this dinner date. If she had to cancel, who knows how long it would take to reschedule.

Before, things were just a mess. Now, they'd become disastrous. What in the world was she going to do to fix this?

Syrae

As though her life wasn't bad enough, after Syrae told her mother she was pregnant, it worsened drastically. She ended up leaving her parents' house – well, actually, she got kicked out. Syrae never understood her mother's decision.

"Pregnant" her mother repeated. "What do you mean you're pregnant?"

"Just what I said, Mom. I'm pregnant. When I didn't get my period, I got concerned. So I bought a pregnancy test. When it came back positive, I bought three more. Whether it was pink, two lines, or a plus, they all gave the same results – I'm positively pregnant!" Syrae shouted. "I *thought* I would be able to have some support when I told you".

"Well, what do you want me to say, Syrae? How am I supposed to feel? My daughter is pregnant with my grandchild – or is it my stepchild? I don't know how to process this".

"Wait – *you* don't know how to process it? What about me? I've had to figure out how to cope with being raped and beaten by my father...a man who is supposed to love me; supposed to protect me. And if that's not devastating enough, I'm carrying his child – and *YOU* don't know how to process this?

I had been doing everything you told me to do to prepare for the future – going to school and getting good grades; I hadn't even had sex until *HE* came along. Now what kid of future am I supposed to have?" Syrae had gotten so worked up that she was totally flushed.

"I just, I just don't know what to do, Syrae. I mean he is your father, and I know what he did to you was terrible and unimaginable, but I love him. I have to figure out what I'm going to do".

Just as her mother finished her sentence, they both heard the door close.

"Percy, is that you?" Syrae's mother yelled.

"Yeah, Hon, it's me" he said as he climbed the stairs.

Syrae's face went pale.

"What's wrong, Syrae?" her mother inquired.

"He doesn't know that I'm pregnant...and I don't want him to know." Syrae replied.

"Well, I think we need to discuss it, Syrae. At least let him know" her mother stated.

Syrae just stood there silently in total disbelief. She couldn't believe her mother thought this was the best way to handle the situation.

Here it is she thought she'd have to stop her mother from killing him; or that they would be packing together to leave, but she wanted to sit down and talk? Talk? To this monster? To the man who annihilated her adolescence?

Absolutely not. She'd done all the talking she planned to do in sharing the news with her mother. And it was clear that no one was capable of comprehending the severity of this situation.

Just as she turned to leave, *HE* entered the room.

"Syrae, what's going on?

Why are you in this room with your mom? I mean..."

Percy couldn't even formulate a complete thought, as he believed himself to be caught. Because of his wife's work schedule and Syrae's school schedule, they were rarely at home at the same time; and when they were, he was typically there to run interference. But how had this gotten past him? What had Syrae told her?

"Percy, can you sit down for a minute?" his wife asked.

"Is everything okay, dear?" he inquired.

"Well, I just finished speaking to Syrae, and she says

she's pregnant".

"Pregnant? How did that happen? Syrae, what do you have to say for yourself? As hard as your mother and I have worked to give you everything, and you go and do something so stupid as to get yourself pregnant! What were you thinking? Answer me!" Percy was irate.

"Get myself pregnant? Get *myself* pregnant? How did it happen? Are you kidding me? All the times you raped me is how. Did you not use condoms?

I'm the youngest one here, and even I know that unprotected sex leads to pregnancy! It's not bad enough that you rape and beat me, but now you have DESTROYED the rest of my life!"

Syrae was so infuriated she could no longer see straight.

"Calm down, Syrae" her mother requested.

"You better tell her to do more than that. No child living under my roof is going to talk to me that way" Percy shouted.

"I don't want to live under your roof. Maybe if I leave, I'll finally be safe and protected – you know, what I *should* have been provided with here!" Syrae shot back.

"Stop it, Syrae" her mother exclaimed. "If you

leave, where will you go?"

"I don't know, but anywhere is better than here" Syrae retorted.

"Let her go to your parents' house" Percy yelled without thinking.

"What does he mean, your parents' house', Mom? You told me that you had no parents. That they died around the time you got pregnant with me. So all of that was a lie? I've had grandparents that could have loved me, that would've been there for me – and you never said a word!" Syrae screamed in disbelief.

"Well, now you know" Percy interrupted. "So get your

stuff and get out!"

"Percy, what are you saying? Don't put her out. And send her to *them*? Don't do this" her mother begged.

"Mom, don't you see?" Syrae began. "This is our ticket out of here. You don't have to stay with him. You don't have to stand for this. We can leave – you and me. We can go to your parents' house. We can have a clean start".

"I can't, Syrae. I can't go back there!" her mother insisted.

"So you'd prefer to stay here with a pedophile rather than live with your parents?"

"Syrae, please stop. Just leave this alone".

"No, Mom, I can't leave it alone. I can't believe you'd choose to be with him knowing what he's done to me. That you can live under the same roof as a rapist!"

"I couldn't – don't you get it? That's why I left. Because I couldn't live under the same roof as a rapist. I never said my parents were dead – I said they were dead to me.

I told my mother what he did to me. I told her about his touches, and she called me a liar! When I got pregnant, she kicked me out and said she never wanted to see me again.

She said she didn't want to see the love child that resulted from her husband's and her daughter's sin. She didn't want to see you, Syrae. So as far as I'm concerned, they died the day I left."

Syrae couldn't believe her ears. Her entire existence was corrupt. Not only had her father raped and impregnated her, but to now find out that history had simply repeated itself was a devastating blow.

Aniyah

Aniyah started making calls early Monday afternoon, as she remembered that her sisters typically didn't work this day of the week. She'd successfully reached her sisters Alicia and Ashley. Both genuinely seemed excited when she told them of her pregnancy, and even happier when presented with the opportunity to reunite at her baby shower!

Aniyah couldn't believe it. She was so ecstatic. Was it really that simple? All she had to do was pick up the phone and make a call? No resistance…no anger…not even a rejection or rebuttal?

Her sisters had actually committed to being there for her – and it wasn't because her mother forced them! Two sisters down, one more to go. She'd left Alexis a voicemail and was now just waiting for her to return the call.

Aniyah was washing the dishes when the phone rang.

"Hello?"

"Hey, it's Alexis. I see you called. What's up?"

Aniyah couldn't determine whether her sister was happy, irritated or what. Her tone was so nonchalant, it was hard to tell. She proceeded with caution when sharing her news.

"I was calling for a couple of reasons. First, I wanted to let you know that I'm pregnant – can you believe it?"

"That's nice" Alexis glumly replied. "What was the other reason you called?"

Aniyah didn't know how to respond to her cold, uncaring reaction. Had Alexis heard her news? Why wasn't she excited to learn that she was going to be an aunt?

The conversation had gone dead when Alexis impatiently repeated herself, "What was the other reason you called?"

"I wanted to invite you to the baby shower I'm having here at the house in a couple of weeks" Aniyah said.

"Oh, well, I won't be able to make it" Alexis stated.

"Without sounding rude, can I ask why not?" Aniyah blurted out.

"I don't owe you any explanations" Alexis snapped.

"But Alicia and Ashley will be here, and I thought it would be an awesome time for us to get together. It would be the first time all of us have been together since, you know, since Mom." Aniyah explained.

After a bit of silence, Alexis said, "Look Aniyah, I'm happy for you. I think you're going to be a great mom. I'm just going through my own stuff right now…"

"Isn't that all the more reason to be with your sisters?" Aniyah interrupted.

"I'm not trying to be mean, but I just can't deal with a baby shower right now, okay?" And with that, Alexis hung up.

Aniyah just stared at the phone in disbelief. Why would her sister treat her that way? Sure, she said she was happy for her, but her actions didn't show it!

She'd given her a compliment in a roundabout sort of way, but that was short-lived with how the conversation ended. Of all the sisters, she and Alexis had always been the closest; so for the life of her, she couldn't understand why Alexis had been so cold.

However, she decided not to allow the negativity to get the best of her. After all, she still had two sisters she could depend on. With that knowledge, she perked up and finished washing the dishes.

As she was wiping down the counters, her husband walked through the door.

"Aniyah, are you home?"

"Yeah, Justin. I'm in the kitchen. How was your day?"

"Same old, same old". Justin replied as he made his way to the kitchen. "What about you? Anything new or different happen today?"

"Well, funny you should ask" Aniyah smirked. "I spoke to my sisters today…"

"Wait, what?" Justin almost choked on the juice he was drinking. "How did that happen? Is everything okay?"

"Justin stop interrupting and let me finish my story. Like I was saying, I called my sisters to tell them about my being pregnant and to invite them to the baby shower".

"Let me guess, they can't make it right?" he asked sarcastically.

"Justin, if you interrupt me one more time" Aniyah remarked with a glaring look. "And for your information, they *ARE* coming…everyone except for Alexis, that is.

I just don't get it, Justin. I wish you could have heard her. She was just so nonchalant about everything – the news and the invitation. She claimed she was happy for me, but in the same breath talked about all she was going through and that she didn't want to deal with a baby shower. Doesn't that seem kind of cold-hearted?" she asked not waiting for his response. "I think I'll call Alicia and ask her take on the situation".

Justin just sat looking confused as his wife walked away still talking, but so muffled that he could barely make out what she was saying. He started to follow her, but figured that she really didn't want his opinion and that he'd served his purpose.

Aniyah made her way back to the living room and picked up the phone to call her sister, Alicia. Her oldest sister was typically everyone's confidant, so if something was going on, surely Alicia would know.

"Hey, sis. It's me again. Do you have a minute?" Aniyah inquired.

"Yeah, what's up?"

"I spoke to Alexis earlier to tell her about the baby and invite her to the shower, and she was kind of rude" Aniyah stated.

"She said she didn't want to come because she couldn't deal with a baby shower right now. I tried to encourage her to come – let her know that all of the sisters would be here, but none of that mattered. I just don't get her, Alicia".

"Don't be too hard on her, Aniyah. She *is* going through a tough time" explained Alicia.

"Well, I would think that coming together would help — especially for a celebration of this magnitude".

"Aniyah, you don't understand. A baby shower is the last thing that Alexis wants to face…"

"Why? What am I missing?"

"You BETTER NOT tell her I told you, or even act like you know for that matter" Alicia said.

"Know what?" she insisted.

"Alexis was pregnant too".

"What? *Was* pregnant?" Aniyah asked confoundedly.

"Yes…*was* pregnant" Alicia continued somberly. "She just suffered a miscarriage two weeks ago and was totally devastated. She couldn't get out of the bed for a week, she was so depressed.

She's still having a hard time coping. I told her to take her time grieving, and maybe even talk to a therapist or something, but you know Alexis. She isn't one to open up and discuss her feelings with a total stranger".

"Or family either for that matter" retorted Aniyah. "I can't believe she didn't tell me".

"Well, we all have a lot going on, but now maybe you can understand why she's not in the mood for a baby shower".

"Yeah, I get it. Thanks, Alicia. I'll talk to you later".

"Okay, bye".

Aniyah couldn't believe it. All of this time she was thinking that her sister was just being rude. All the while, Alexis was just suffering in silence.

To make matters worse, she probably unknowingly caused Alexis to relive the agony by sharing her news. She did not want her sister to go through this alone. She was determined to come up with a plan to help – even if that meant cancelling her baby shower.

Barbara

A few weeks had passed since their last counseling session, and things were still quite tense between she and Charles. It seemed like anything – everything that was said would stir up memories. And of course, every movie that came on was about someone cheating; even the Christian movies had one of the spouses involved in an affair.

More than anything, Barbara simply wanted to be happy. She wanted to figure out a way to rekindle the love that originally brought them together.

There were times, over the course

of these last eight years, where Charles confessed his love for Barbara. He told her how he could never imagine his life without her; and Lord knows, she felt the same. In fact, it was her love and determination that kept her going.

They laughed together. They cried together. They were working on improving their communication (which was one of the elements that initially plagued their relationship). It wasn't always bad times; but when the times were bad, they were bad.

Charles would experience bouts of depression. There were days that he couldn't force himself out of bed. It never appeared to be any rhyme or reason for the episodes. When he felt bad, he'd lash out at Barbara.

He would not just bring up the affair, but he would want her to relive every grueling detail. Although Barbara felt that this only made matters worse, she felt conflicted. She didn't want to add further pain, but she didn't want to anger him. When he got in those moods, there was no getting around discussing the issue. And today was one of those days.

"Barbara, can you come here for a minute?"

"Yeah, babe. I'm on my way. Do you need me to bring you anything?"

"No. I just need you to come help me".

Help him? What could have happened? Barbara wondered. She knew that Charles hadn't been feeling well and hoped he hadn't fallen out of bed. As she made her way to her husband, she belted out, "Charles, where are you? Are you okay?"

"I'm fine" he said as he was coming out of the bathroom. "But what I need you to do is help me understand what it was that a total stranger could give to you that you couldn't get from me".

"Baby, we've gone over this a thousand times. I don't know what you want me to say" Barbara said in a low voice, hanging her head.

"*I want you to answer the question*" Charles replied. "*You said that this was just some random guy you met in a grocery store. So, how is it that you got comfortable enough to sleep with him? That doesn't just happen*".

"*Well as I've told you before, Charles, it was just a natural progression of things. We'd been married for over a decade, and there was no more spark. I mean, not even a flicker*".

"*How can you say that, Barbara?*" asked a perplexed Charles. "*We had an active sex life, so how can you say that the spark was gone?*"

"You still equate sex and love" she helplessly explained. "Sure we were having sex, but we'd long stopped being intimate with one another. There were no hugs, no kisses. Many days, we didn't even speak; you were working and I was home helping the kids.

It had been years since we'd gone out on a date, or had any time alone for that matter. And even when we had sex, it felt awkward because I no longer felt connected. You never had time for me. Whenever I'd ask if we could spend time together, you'd turn me down saying that there was something more important you needed to do. So after years of asking, begging and pleading just to continuously be ignored and refused, I gave up.

I didn't go out looking for him — I mean, yeah, I did go back to thank him that first time, but that was really it. When we saw each other at the restaurant, it was unbelievable to me how well we hit it off. Even then, I wasn't sizing him up; I just thought that I'd acquired a friend.

Weeks had gone by before I saw him at the store again. When I did, he told me that he had something to tell me, but he didn't have time to share it at work, so he asked if it would be okay if he called me. I didn't see it as being problematic, so I gave him my number.

He'd just found out that his

brother was terminally ill, and remembered me telling him about my sister. He thought that if anyone could understand his feelings, it would be me.

So we talked on the phone once or twice a month, whenever he needed encouragement. After a while, we began meeting because he felt overwhelmed by the situation. Everything was legitimately platonic during those times. I was just trying to help a friend make it through a difficult period. I could never share it with you, Charles, because you were never home…and when you were, you'd just shirk me off.

Although I was helping to encourage him, I found myself

looking forward to our outings. It was adult conversation with someone who actually enjoyed my company. He didn't shush me — he actually welcomed my opinions. He laughed at my jokes; he appreciated my time. I had totally forgot how that felt.

But anyway, within a few months, his brother's health began taking a toll for the worse. When he died, I called to extend my condolences. I could tell that he wasn't handling it well. So one day, I offered to come over to help cheer him up.

We talked for awhile and watched movies until we both fell asleep. I got up to leave, and hugged him goodbye. However, the hug turned into a kiss, and the kiss turned into – well, you know the rest".

"Yeah, I know the rest" mumbled an exasperated Charles.

"But Charles, it was only that one time. We both immediately knew that we'd gone too far. I got caught up in the moment. Charles, I am so sorry, and have been for the last eight years. You have no idea how hard it is for me to look at myself in the mirror; the guilt and shame I feel every time I look at you. How difficult it is for me to look at you knowing that I hurt you.

I didn't mean to hurt you. I

didn't even mean to do it. It was simply a moment of weakness. I felt so guilty that I came home and confessed.

You're the one I love. You're the one that has my heart. I just want you to love me the way you once did. Pay attention to me. Talk to me. Cherish me.

I know that I messed up. But I know that we can work through this. Do you truly believe that, Charles?"

"Yes, I do, Barbara. I do want to get over this. I don't want the infidelity to be a constant thought in my mind. I just need you to help me".

"Well, Charles, we have to make a conscious effort to move forward.

It's not helping us to keep looking in the past because it doesn't change what happened. All it does is destroy whatever progress we do manage to make".

"I know" he said. "It just scares me that I almost lost you. You're the best thing that ever happened to me, Barbara" he stated while passionately embracing her.

"I feel the same way. I never want to be without you".

"You never will be" he replied. He gazed into her eyes and began to kiss her. Barbara smiled inside as this was the first time in eight years that they had been able to rekindle their fire.

Monique

It was Thursday, and Monique still hadn't told her parents about her dinner date with Jeff – much less that it was scheduled for the same day and time as their family outing. She finally convinced herself to just tell them. "Stop trying to figure out how to do it, and simply say it" she repeated to herself. She had already wasted two days, and at this point, time was of the essence.

"Mom, Dad, are you guys here?" Monique shouted.

It was still early, so she was hoping to catch them before they'd left for work.

"Yeah, honey, we're in the kitchen" her mom responded.

"Here goes nothing" Monique mumbled under her breath.

"Good morning" Monique started. "I have something I have to tell you guys".

"What's going on, Monique?" her dad inquired.

"Well, I know that we we're supposed to be going out tomorrow night to see a movie, but I kinda double-booked myself without knowing it. I already planned to meet with Jeff for dinner and Mom, when you came in my room the other day...I just, I mean, things had already been tense between us, and I want us to go out, but I really want to meet

Jeff".

"It's alright, Monique" her mom interrupted. "We understand, and it's okay. Bill and I will just go out on our own date, Friday" her mom said giving her dad a wink.

"Yeah, we can go out another time" Bill added. "We simply wanted to make sure that everything between the three of us was still in tact. As long as you're okay, so are we. Go, enjoy yourself. And we want to hear all about it on Saturday".

"Sure thing" Monique responded as she hugged her parents and kissed them each on the cheek. "I have to go to class, but I'll see you guys later. Love you…and thanks!"

Monique couldn't believe that everything worked out so smoothly. Her parents weren't upset and she
didn't have to cancel her dinner plans with Jeff. All she had to do was get through her Psychology class today and she could spend the rest of her time prepping for tomorrow night.

The time seemed to fly by; although it was her freshman year in college, she transitioned from high school fairly well. She took four classes per semester – Psychology and Math on Tuesdays and Thursdays; English and Linguistics on Mondays and Wednesdays.

Monique always enjoyed school, and college was no

different. Of all her classes, Psychology was her favorite. It was just something about Freud and his ideologies that she absolutely loved.

Once she made it home, she checked her social media accounts to make sure that Jeff hadn't tried to contact her or cancel, and he hadn't. Monique was so excited and anxious she could barely make it through her day. She even went to bed early; it wasn't quite nine o'clock when she turned out the lights.

She couldn't seem to sleep. She tossed and turned constantly. When she finally did get to sleep, she kept having nightmares. In one dream, she was in a field running, calling Jeff's name, and the next thing she knew, she was falling off of a cliff. Monique woke up right before she hit the ground.

No sooner than she went back to sleep, she was running through that same field calling for Jeff, but this time she fell. When she looked down, she could tell she was in a cemetery staring at Jeff's tombstone. Again, Monique awoke totally shaken and determined not to go back to sleep.

She sat straight up, reached for the remote control and turned on the television. It was three in the morning, and nothing was on. A few moments later, she heard a gentle knock on her door.

"Monique, are you okay?"

It was her mother. Apparently, her nightmares had disturbed the entire house.

"Yeah, Mom. I'm fine. Just having a little trouble sleeping."

"Did you want to talk about it?" her mom asked as she let herself in the room.

"I just can't seem to sleep" Monique explained. She recounted her nightmares to her mother.

"It seems like meeting your father has you more anxious than you're letting on...but you can never fool your subconscious – isn't that what you once told me?"

She and Monique both laughed.

"I am a bit nervous, Mom, I can't lie. I have tons of mixed feelings. What if he doesn't want to answer my questions? What if I don't like the answers he gives? Is tomorrow going to be the first and only time I see him? Is he only meeting me because I asked, or does he want to begin an actual relationship with me? Do I call him Jeff, or should I call him Dad?"

"No wonder you can't sleep" her mother remarked. "Your mind is running a mile a minute. Lie back down, take a deep breath and relax. Everything is going to be fine. It's going to work out the way it's supposed to work out.

Let the conversation flow naturally...just talk to him. If you want or feel like calling him Dad, then do so; if not, call him Jeff. Don't put so much pressure on yourself. I'm sure he's probably nervous too!

But remember, he agreed to meet you, which means that he wants to get to know you. I'm sure he's going to be excited to talk to you and answer any and all of your questions".

"Thanks, Mom. You always know just what to say".

"Well, I try" she replied jokingly. "Now, let's just say a quick prayer so we both can get some sleep".

Monique loved how her mom was always capable of understanding her. She always gave the best advice. After that talk and prayer, Monique slept like a baby.

It was almost two o'clock in

the afternoon when Monique woke up. She couldn't believe her eyes when she saw the clock. She quickly jumped out of bed and headed for the kitchen.

How could she have slept so late? Maybe she was more tired than she thought. It was good that she didn't have classes on Fridays; otherwise, she would've missed or been extremely late.

When she got to the kitchen, she noticed a note on the refrigerator:

"Monique, both Dad and I have to work late today. You were sleeping so soundly that we didn't want to wake you. By the time we get home, you'll probably be gone. We love you. Have a great time…and relax! Love you, Mom"

Monique found herself comforted by her mother's words. She only had a few hours before time to go. She decided that she would leave close to six since she was taking the bus.

Travel times were typically longer in the evenings and she wanted to make sure she arrived promptly. She'd already selected her outfit the day before. She decided that she would eat, shower, and then watch television and relax until time to get dressed and go.

Syrae

Sitting alone in the waiting area of the emergency room, Syrae began to look around. The walls were lifeless – no pictures, no paintings – nothing to even try to conceal its appearance. Just ugly and barren for the world to see. The paint was dull and had begun to chip away.

Suddenly, Syrae noticed that these walls were symbolic of her life. Ugly was the way she felt; barren was her state of being; and as a result of her past, she was dull, and her life chipped away. If only she could turn back the hands of time.

Syrae remembered leaving her parents' home – alone and devastated...and for more reasons than one. While she was glad to learn that Percy was not her biological father, the truth wasn't much better because either way she looked at it, her father was a rapist.

It broke her heart to learn that her mother had endured the same trauma; but, because she had gone through similar experiences, Syrae could not understand how her mother could abandon her. How could she choose to stay with him instead of leave with her own daughter?

Although she remained conflicted, she did her best to

make peace with the situation. She determined the best thing to do was to have an abortion. She figured that this cycle of abuse would end with her.

Syrae admired her mother's courage and that she could have her under those circumstances. However, she didn't possess that strength. All she could think of was what happened if she got involved with someone like her mother and grandmother? She would never be able to forgive herself if something happened to her child and she did nothing to help.

In her mind, the decision seemed logical and straight-forward, but when she had the procedure done, things went terribly wrong. She didn't know that in having the abortion she would end up with an infection. And that this infection would lead to her having fertility issues. The doctors told her that she'd never be able to have children again.

Talk about hind sight. Had she known that legally aborting one baby would cost her the gift of motherhood altogether, she definitely would have given it more thought. But Syrae concluded that it just wasn't in the cards for her to be a mother. After that incident, she reconciled with her mother, but she knew that she could never forgive Percy.

Syrae ended up staying in a shelter for teens. She couldn't go home, and she figured it best not to pursue her grandparents. After learning that her grandfather was actually her father, Syrae didn't want to see him, and was pretty sure that he didn't want to see her.

She dropped out of high school – a decision that to this day, she still regrets. With all the stress she'd gone through at home, she just couldn't focus anymore. While at school, her attention was always somewhere else. She'd been separated herself from her friends, and after things ended at home the way they did, Syrae was alone and left to fend for herself.

She had to make sure she had food to eat and somewhere to sleep. She was now totally responsible for her own well-being. So going to school was no longer a top priority.

It was while at the shelter that Syrae learned how to make money. Her roommate, Tiffany, explained, "The only person you can count on in this world is you. So you have to use what you have to get what you want. And if you don't want to be in here for the next three years, you need to get some money and start saving...that's what I've been doing."

Tiffany was the only one Syrae really got along with at the shelter. Although Tiffany was a year older, she was easy to talk to, and seemed genuinely concerned about her. So when she asked Tiffany how she made her money, she invited Syrae to go with her on her next date. Looking back, she was so naïve, but heck, she was only 16.

Syrae and Tiffany got ready to meet Tiffany's "friends", Jake and Steven. Tiffany said they were supposed to take a train to meet them at a restaurant. When they arrived, Syrae noticed the guys were in different cars. So the first thought she had was, "Why didn't they pick us up if they BOTH have vehicles?"

She decided that maybe Tiffany was ashamed that they lived in a shelter. But then, she noticed that not only were they *not* getting out of their cars, but they had began blowing their horns and motioning for the girls to come to them. That's when Syrae decided to speak up:

"Um, Tiff, if we're supposed to meet them at the restaurant, why are they not getting out?"

"Oh, I never said we were going IN the restaurant" Tiffany explained. "This is where we're meeting them".

"To do what?" Syrae asked.

"Girl, are you really that

clueless?" Tiffany responded. After looking at Syrae's face, she realized that she was indeed. "Look, you remember when I said that you have to use what you have to get what you want? Well, I was talking about your body."

"Wait, what? You expect for me to make out with some guy I don't even know?" Syrae remembered asking.

"Uh, yeah. And if you want the big bucks, you'll do more than just make out!"

Syrae must have looked totally confused because Tiffany followed up with, "Look, I wouldn't tell you to do something that I thought was dangerous. This isn't a permanent way of life...it's just a quick way to make some real money. You don't always want to live in a shelter, do you? So, hey, you gotta do what you gotta do."

And with that, she waved and said, "I'll see you soon. Enjoy your night".

Syrae just stood there dumbfounded. Was this what she signed up for? To be a prostitute? Absolutely not. But Tiffany did have a point. She didn't want to be in a shelter for the rest of her life. She dropped out of high school, so it wasn't like she had people standing in line to hire her.

Even though she'd forgiven her mother, she hadn't seen or heard from her in months. And she had made it crystal clear that she wasn't leaving Percy, and there was no way that Syrae was going to live with him.

The more she thought about it, she really didn't have much choice. She had to do something to make money. And like Tiffany said, it didn't have to be permanent – just something to help her get to the next stage of life.

The honk of the horn interrupted Syrae's thoughts.

"Are you coming?" the guy yelled from his car.

Was this Steven or Jake? She didn't know. But just then, it began to rain so she made a run for it.

"Hi, I'm Syrae".

"Yeah, I'm Steven. It took you long enough. Are we going to do this or what?"

"Oh great" Syrae thought to herself. "A real jerk".

The next thing she knew, he had his hands all over her, touching her in ways she hated – ways that reminded her of Percy. Then, he pulled up her skirt. As he climbed on top of her, it was all she could do to hold back the tears. She was totally numb – no feelings – just empty.

This should have been devastating, but she'd already gone through it before. So she knew how to pick up the pieces and act as though nothing happened. When he finished, he flung $200 at her and told her to leave.

"It doesn't seem like that was seven years ago" Syrae whispered, shaking her head.

At that moment, she noticed the doctor standing in the waiting area calling her name, "Ms. Turner, she's awake. You can see her now".

Aniyah

Two weeks had passed, and Aniyah was still having a hard time processing the fact that her sister had suffered a miscarriage. She wasn't necessarily upset that Alexis hadn't shared it with her, but just knowing she was going through such a traumatic time by herself broke Aniyah's heart. She couldn't even begin to imagine the devastation – the pain – her sister was enduring.

She had now made it her mission to reunite her sisters, not for her baby shower, but to serve as comfort and support for Alexis. She called Alicia first with her proposal.

"So, Alicia, I was thinking that maybe you could call Alexis and ask her to come over to your house" Aniyah started.

"And why would I do that?" Alicia asked.

"Well, obviously, Alexis is comfortable talking to you, and she would be more likely to say 'yes' to you than any of the rest of us" explained Aniyah.

"You and Alexis were always the close ones" Alicia reminded Aniyah.

"Uh, yeah, I thought so too, but apparently, I was wrong".

"And why would you say that?" Alicia questioned.

"Alicia, she had a miscarriage and she didn't tell me about it – she told you. And although I'm glad she had someone to talk to, I can't say that I'm not hurt that she didn't think she could talk to me about it".

"Aniyah, the reason Alexis

came to me was because she knew that I could relate to her experience" Alicia pointed out.

"What are you talking about?" Aniyah asked totally clueless.

Taking a deep breath, Alicia responded, "The reason why I dropped out of high school, Aniyah, was because I got pregnant. When I found out, I was so terrified of what Mom would do if she found out, that I made sure she never would…I had an abortion.

But, I still ended up having to tell her because I had some complications afterwards and I didn't know what was going on with me *or* my body. I thought I was dying, I was in so much pain. When I told Mom about my symptoms, she asked if I'd been pregnant. Aniyah, this was over 10 years ago, and Mom's gone, but I promise I still feel goosebumps on my arms that I felt when she asked me that question. And you know none of us were ever any good lying to Mom, so I told her everything – about the pregnancy, the abortion, my fear – everything.

Mom began crying, but it wasn't for the reasons I thought. When I apologized for being a disappointment, she looked at me in total disbelief and asked, 'Is that why you think I'm crying? I can assure you that it's not, Alicia'. You know how Mom talked.

She told me that she was crying because I felt that it was better to hurt myself than to tell her. She said that although she may have been strict, she only wanted the best for us. That it was never her intention to make us feel that we couldn't come to her for whatever the situation.

Aniyah, I cried so hard

because never in a million years did I think that Mom would understand. We ended up going to the doctor to get me together, but needless to say, our relationship was never the same. After that, I didn't just see her as my mother; I saw her as my friend. Lord knows I miss that woman".

"Wow" was all that Aniyah could manage to utter.

"Wow" she repeated.

"I had no clue about any of this, Alicia. How could I have *NO CLUE* about any of this?" Aniyah was truly dumbfounded.

"Aniyah, don't beat yourself up too much" Alicia comforted. "You were still in grammar school when it happened, and you know we never discussed personal business publicly. Mom didn't feel the need to tell you guys; she simply encouraged me to learn from my mistake, and get my life together. So that's what I've been trying my best to do.

But the point is, somewhere along the line, Alexis heard something about what happened to me – I don't know how and I didn't ask – and although she didn't know the whole story, she knew enough to believe that she could come to me and that I would understand."

"All of this is so unbelievable" Aniyah said. "I mean, all this time...I knew nothing. And you're right, you could definitely give Alexis a perspective that I never could. All I would have been able to do was provide a shoulder; and the truth is, sometimes that's not enough."

"Look at who's sounding so wise and mature" Alicia teased.

"I've always been understanding, Alicia".

"Well, that may be the case, but...never mind" Alicia stopped herself.

"What were going to say?" Alicia asked.

"Nope. I don't want to ruin what we've got going" Alicia replied.

"Please, Alicia" begged Aniyah. If I can't get the truth from you, who else will tell me? I'm a big girl - I can handle it."

"Aniyah, you're right. You are a nice person and most people pick up on that relatively quickly. And I'm proud of all the choices you've made in and for your life. But sometimes it just seems like you TRY SO HARD to be perfect.

I mean, I know that sounds crazy, but it's like sometimes you don't come across as authentic.

Everything about your life has been textbook, so it kinda makes it impossible for those of us who make mistakes to be able to relate to you. And that's why us sisters stopped trying a long time ago.

It's not like we were rooting for you to fail, but how could we, a high school dropout; a single mother; and an unsuccessful entrepreneur - how could we identify with you? Every place we failed, you succeeded; so there's nothing that we really even have in common."

"What about love, Alicia? Shouldn't love be the force that drives us together? Shouldn't our love for each other - and for Mom - shouldn't that be enough regardless of our differences?

I mean, I get what you're saying, and no, I never thought about it like that, but why would or should my accomplishments alienate me from my sisters? And you're right, the bulk of my life *was* lived to please Mom...I realized that the day she died. But you guys were totally instrumental in my success. You may believe that you failed, but through that failure I learned what to do.

I've never thought of myself as better than you guys. In fact, I'm so proud of how you all have been able to turn your lives around DESPITE your trials. I tell people about my sisters all the time".

"Now, I'm speechless. Aniyah, I never knew you felt that way. You're proud of u But why? We don't have any degrees, or 6-figure salaries, or any of the things that you have".

"I'm proud of you because of who you are, Alicia. Real love - true love - has nothing to do with materialistic possessions. Those things can come and go; but our love can last us a lifetime".

"Wow. You really are wise beyond your years" Alicia complimented.

"Well, since we're being honest, I can't take credit for that last part. That was something Mom told me a long time ago...I just never forgot it!"

"I thought it sounded familiar!"

Both sisters laughed.

"Now ge back to my plan. I think we can make it happen. You just get Alexis to your house and I will work on Ashley. I'm sure once she hears the 'why' she will be on board. It's time for a good old-fashioned sleepover. You remember the fun we used to have when we were kids?"

"Yeah, I remember" Alicia chimed in.

"Well, let's not just relive those memories; let's make some new ones. It's time."

"It's been time" Alicia added.

Barbara

The next morning, Barbara opened her eyes to find Charles missing. Assuming that he was in the bathroom, she closed her eyes and began to reflect on the previous night of passion. She could tell that it was a new beginning for them.

It had been such a long time since they'd been intimate on that level. Charles had always been a good lover, but for Barbara that wasn't enough. She wanted to know - to feel - his love for her and she definitely received what she'd been hoping for.

At that moment, she opened her eyes again realizing her husband had yet to return. A concerned Barbara rushed to her feet, put on her robe and began searching for her husband.

"Charles," she began calling out as she roamed throughout the house. She knocked on the bathroom door - no response. She opened the door to be sure, but Charles was not there. She began to head downstairs still calling his name - this time a bit more anxiously.

"Charles, where are you?" Barbara belted out, but no reply. She went to the living room - no Charles. She looked in the kitchen - no Charles. The downstairs bathroom - still no Charles.

"Now if he's not in the den..."

Barbara whispered.

By this time, she was worried and moving swiftly. As she approached the door, she noticed it was closed. She found this to be odd because in all the years they'd lived in that house, the door had NEVER been closed.

A worried Barbara slowly opened the door, afraid of what she might find. To her surprise, she found her husband...on his knees - praying.

This really threw Barbara for a loop because Charles had never been a spiritual man, religious maybe, but never spiritual. She'd often described Charles that way to her family and would always have to explain the difference even to them.

"Going to church makes you religious; having a relationship with God makes you spiritual".

Whether or not it was an accurate description for others didn't matter to Barbara because she knew what she meant. Through the years they'd go to church, mainly on special days - Christmas; Easter; maybe Mother's Day - you know, the days that it seemed like the thing to do. And of course, whenever someone got married; a baby was christened; or a friend passed away; they'd be in attendance for those occasions.

But there was never a time when Barbara could remember seeing her husband pray. Heck, he'd get frustrated if she asked him to say grace over their meals. But now, he was praying.

Barbara found herself standing at the door completely frozen. She immediately got a sinking feeling in the pit of her stomach. She didn't know if something happened to one of the children, or if a family member died.

"Oh my goodness, what if he lost his job and doesn't know how to tell me" she wondered aloud.

The possibilities seemed endless. Just as Barbara began to get overwhelmed with her thoughts, she noticed her husband rising to his feet.

"You startled me, dear" Charles said. "What are you doing? Why are you just standing there?" he questioned.

"Charles, honey, what's wrong? You can tell me. I promise whatever it is, I'll be strong. We can get through it together".

He looked at his wife totally baffled.

"Sweetheart, what are you talking about?"

"Don't take this the wrong way, Charles, but I've NEVER seen you pray before. So the way I figure, something must be terribly wrong"

Barbara explained.

"Well, you figured wrong" he stated. "Honey, after the night we had, I knew I owed God at least a 'Thank You'. I realize I probably haven't prayed as often as I should, but Barbara, I pray.

The state of our marriage had me praying a lot. You may not have seen me, but trust me when I say I was praying. When you had the affair was when I really began.

As hurt as I was, I knew I didn't want to lose you. And the truth is, I may have never admitted it to you, but I know that to some degree, my actions caused your reactions. That truth is never easy to accept. For so long, I blamed you because I didn't want to hear, much less acknowledge, that I could have been responsible for how you felt.

My initial prayers were what led me to seek counseling. The problem was that I stopped praying for awhile because I was so hurt with what was said in those sessions. I mean, I tried to participate, tried to engage, but whenever we got too deep, my defenses went up.

After weeks of tension, I would pray and ask God to help me - help us - to get better; once we did, my curiosity would get the best of me. I'd start asking questions and before I knew it, we'd be right back in the same bitter place. It got to the point that I didn't really want to pray anymore because it felt like it wasn't helping. It was a constant roller coaster ride - and Barbara, you know how much I HATE roller coasters.

But after last night, I don't know. It's like, I know God had to have done something because I replayed it in my head. I saw where the conversation could have gone the wrong way - because in the past, it typically had gone the wrong way - but this time, we moved beyond it.

We were able to focus on our love for each other. our feelings as they are in the here and now. And baby, I don't know, it just did something to me. All these years I allowed myself to be distracted by what honestly doesn't even matter.

Because the bottom line is that I love you and I don't want to know a life that doesn't have you in it. And it just clicked. Something inside of me said, 'Now just let it go and move on. Don't waste your time dwelling on the past. Focus on making memories for your future'.

Barbara, you are my future. All I can do is apologize for how I made you feel back then, and even with the conversation I drug you through now causing you to relive your pain. I'm ready to move forward".

Barbara just stood there looking at her husband in amazement. She couldn't believe all the things that came pouring out. She hadn't heard that much truth and sincerity in eight years of counseling. She could look at him and tell that he wasn't putting on a show. She knew that he genuinely meant every word.

"Oh, Charles" was all she managed to utter.

She embraced him and gave a passionate kiss. In that kiss, Barbara remembered all the nights she cried, wishing her husband could see how much she loved him. That he could understand that it was a mistake. That the only man she ever *truly loved was him.*

She knew that her actions would create consequences - and had no problem taking accountability. However, to have to constantly be made to relive her actions - to be asked to provide a sensible explanation for an irrational decision it always proved to end in disaster.

The truth was she couldn't explain it away...no matter how much Charles pressed her. She knew it was wrong, and she knew she would never do it again. She just had no idea how to make her husband believe her. She no longer considered herself to even be in the same realm as the person she was when the affair happened.

For so long her deepest desire was that her husband could truly accept her feelings, her truth. And now, it seemed that he finally had. Barbara stopped, stared into Charles' eyes and replied, "I'm ready to move forward too".

Monique

It was ten minutes to seven when Monique arrived. When she entered, the waitress escorted her to her table. She was surprised to see a gentleman already seated.

"Jeff?"

"Upon hearing his name, he dropped his menu, looked at Monique, and rose to his feet to greet her. When she looked at him, she smiled and they hugged as though they'd both been waiting for that moment.

As they returned to their seats, Monique noticed that small talk came very naturally. She wondered if the entire night would go this well because she did anticipate asking some questions that may prove awkward.

When dinner was over, Jeff suggested that they go for a walk in a nearby park so they'd have an opportunity to talk a bit more. It was as though he knew what Monique was thinking.

"I just want to thank you again for agreeing to meet me" he started. "I know you probably have some questions for me, and I want to be able to give you my undivided attention".

"Well, since you mentioned it, I do have some things I want to say to you. I have a lot of mixed feelings" Monique explained.

"What do you mean?" Jeff

asked.

"I mean, I really did enjoy dinner and I'm grateful that I had the opportunity to meet you, but, why now? Why after 18 years? Do you understand how confusing life has been for me? I mean, in the back of my mind, I knew I was different – that I didn't belong, but I could never quite put my finger on it. That is until Mom told me that Bill wasn't my biological father.

And then it was like all of these feelings just came rushing at once. The void I'd always felt became even bigger. I just, for the life of me, I couldn't – I don't understand why you would never want to see me.

Monique

I can understand how at the time when Mom got pregnant with me you might not have been ready for a family, but you never wondered about me? You never wanted to know what happened to me? I don't think you truly understand how much it hurts to know that your own father didn't want you.

Didn't want to be part of your life. It just makes you wonder all types of things about yourself. Like, were you ashamed of me? Was I not good enough for you?

Monique just broke down. She had no idea that she would get so worked up. Jeff just looked at his daughter with tears in his own eyes. He didn't quite know how to respond.

"It was never that you were not good enough for me, or that I was ashamed of you. I respected your mother's decision to have you, and once I found out that she and Bill were happy together, I thought you'd be better off. He was a good guy, and she was happy, and I knew together they could provide a more stable life for you.

I travelled a lot, so I was never in one place very long. In fact, I just recently left that job, which is the reason I'm back in Chicago. You have to believe me, I thought about you all the time. And when I saw you reached out to me on social media, it felt like an answered prayer".

"That's exactly how I felt when you responded" said Monique.

"I was so happy to know that not only would I get a chance to meet you, but I could finally get rid of all of this weight I've been carrying around. I resented you for a long time…well, if I'm being honest, I hated you. And it's crazy because it's like, how can you hate someone that you don't know? But I did because I felt like because of your absence in my life, I couldn't truly love myself as I should have because all I could see was hurt.

I prayed every night, all I could say was 'Love Me, Please'.

And at first, I thought those words were geared toward you, but I learned that they were actually geared toward myself. I had to find a way to dig past the hurt and love myself anyway. I had to stop allowing this situation to hold me hostage. And although I was making some progress, tonight has really helped me heal more than you will ever know. So even if I never see you again..."

"Please, don't finish that sentence" Jeff interrupted. "I would really love if we could find a way to get to know each other better. I've already missed all these years; I really don't want to miss another day".

"I so agree" Monique smiled.

"It seems like finally all of the pieces of my life are coming together. Thanks, Dad".

Syrae

Syrae crept slowly into the room, afraid of what her eyes were going to behold. Receiving a phone call to inform her that she'd been in an accident – and had coded...it made Syrae realize just how much she truly loved her.

"Mom", she called as she entered.

Her mother turned her head at the sound of her daughter's voice. Syrae could see tears on her mother's face, which matched her own. She really didn't know what to say, and it appeared the feeling for her mother was mutual.

At that moment, her mother extended her arm, reaching for her daughter. Syrae dropped her purse and ran to her bedside. The two released even more tears as they embraced for the first time in almost 10 years.

"What happened, Mom?" Syrae finally managed to ask.

"Percy and I were out driving and we, we began to argue. He was yelling and had taken his eyes off the road, and ended up running through the red light. And next thing I knew, we were hearing the horn of a semi-truck.

I screamed for him to hit the brakes, but it was too late.

The next thing I knew, I was waking up here. I don't even remember what we were arguing about...Oh my God, where is he? Where is Percy?"

Syrae hung her head, avoiding eye contact with her mom.

"Um, Mom, I don't know how to tell you this, but...um, he didn't make it."

"Syrae, what are you saying?"

"Well, the hospital called to notify me about the accident. They told me that you were touch and go for awhile, but Percy didn't make it".

Her mother began crying

again; however, she took the news better than Syrae imagined.

"You know, Syrae, I don't know how long I'm going to be in the hospital. With two broken legs, I'm sure it's going to be awhile. And, even beyond that, when they do discharge me, I'm sure I'll need a hand around the house. Is there any chance that you could come back home? I know it may be an inconvenience..."

Mom, I'd love to" Syrae joyfully responded. "The truth is I've missed you so much. Over the past few years, there were so many times I wanted to pick up the phone – wanted to hear your voice, but I allowed my pride and hurt and fear to stop me. And then when I got the call my heart sank because I thought...well, it doesn't matter what I thought. Let's just say that I've never been so glad to be wrong in my life.

And when I heard about what happened to Percy, I thought I'd be happy or at least have a sense of relief after what he did to me. But I was actually sad. Not because I missed him, but because I knew you'd be devastated."

"Syrae, it does hurt, I can't lie. But you know I always try to find the good out of every situation. And the way I see it, it took me to become broken, literally, in order to have an opportunity to get healed. I may have lost my husband, but now I have the chance to restore my relationship with my daughter".

"Mom, I would love that. I've done a lot of things in my life that I haven't been proud of, all because I was trying to fill a void. I was looking for love – trying to figure out if I was even worthy to be loved. Everywhere I turned, everything I did, it seemed the answer was a resounding 'NO'.

I used to pray every night, 'Love Me...Please'. I cried out repeatedly wanting you to love me. Thinking that if you loved me, my life would be different. Feeling that if you saw my pain it would motivate you to love me. I felt as long as we had each other, we could conquer the world. However, the fact is that my pain didn't motivate you as I thought.

I ended up making a lot of bad decisions trying to figure out life and love. Along the way, I discovered a few things:
1)Love means different things to different people.
2)Everyone does not show love the same.
3)People value love differently.

Perhaps one of the most important lessons I learned was that you loved me the best way you knew how. That's why I could forgive you then, and why I want to move forward with you now.

I don't want to keep allowing my past to determine the decisions I make for my future. My hope is that in rebuilding my relationship with you it will help me to not only love you, but it will help me to finally figure out how to love me too!"

Aniyah

Aniyah was so excited. She'd contacted Ashley, and just as she thought, once her sistr knew the plan, she was totally on board. Aniyah had been going on and on about it to Justin; she just couldn't contain her excitement.

"Justin, can you believe it? Can you believe that the girls and I are finally getting back together after all this time? I knew if I just held out hope that it would happen again" she continued ecstatically.

"Well, I'm happy you're happy, Aniyah. I just don't want you to get too happy. What happens if they bail out on you? It has happened before" Justin reminded.

"Look, Justin, I know you mean

well, and I get what you're saying, but I'm telling you this time is going to be different - I can feel it".

"Well, as long as you don't get hurt again..."

"I'll be fine, Justin. Stop worrying. Sometimes you just have to have a little faith. You'll be surprised how far it will take you".

Aniyah sang as she packed her bag.

Justin looked on in amazement. His wife was so incredible; she was always able to bounce back from hurt and disappointment as though it was nothing. He recalled all the unanswered invitations. He remembered all the nights his wife cried herself to sleep - not knowing, not understanding why her sisters had seemingly abandoned her. And to look at her now, you'd never know she'd seen a bad day.

"You're so awesome" Justin told his wife as he kissed her goodbye. "So I'll see you tomorrow?"

"Yes, babe. Ashley is going to pick me up and then we're heading straight to Alicia's house".

"Enjoy yourself, sweetheart. I love you". And with that he left for work.

Aniyah had finished making her preparations for the sleepover and decided to get her housework done while she waited for her sister to arrive. Ashley was rarely on time, so she knew she'd also probably have time to take a nap before leaving.

Aniyah jumped up from the couch. "What time is it?" she asked aloud.

She reached for her phone and

was shocked to see it was after 3pm. Ashley was supposed to have picked her up over an hour ago. She checked her phone to see if she missed a call or had a voicemail; neither was the case. She called Ashley's phone and it went straight to voicemail.

"Great" Aniyah thought. "Her phone must be dead".

Aniyah remained calm. She decided to call Alicia to see if she'd heard from Ashley. Unfortunately, she didn't have any good news. Not only had Alicia not heard from Ashley, but she told her that Alexis had called and said that she wasn't sure if she was going to be able to make it.

"Oh no, everything is all falling apart. I was sure this time would be different" Aniyah thought to herself.

She headed for the stairs. She figured that she might as well unpack her things.

"Maybe it's just not meant to be" she mumbled.

Aniyah tried to stay positive, but she'd been down this road too many times to count. And for that reason, you'd think she'd be used to the feeling; however, she couldn't help but feel disappointed.

As soon as she reached the bedroom, the doorbell rang. "Why does it seem like people wait until I get all the way up the stairs before they want to ring that bell? Don't they know I'm pregnant?" she fussed.

The doorbell rang again, and then again. "I'm coming" she yelled as if whoever it was could hear her.

When she opened the door, no

one was there. "Are you kidding me?" she screamed. Just as she was about to close the door, she heard a familiar voice holler, "Don't close the door".

She turned to see Ashley running toward her. Aniyah smiled so big it seemed to have made the sun shine brighter.

"Ashley" she shrieked joyfully.

"Hey, girl, I'm sorry for being late. I got a flat on the way over. I tried calling, but my phone died and I forgot my charger. I had to go back to pay the meter just now because although I don't think we'll be long, with the day I've had, I didn't want to chance it. You know what Mom used to say, 'Some days it seems like anything that can go wrong...will go wrong' Aniyah chimed in.

The sisters stared at each

other and laughed. No matter how much time passed in between visits, they always remained in sync.

"Girl, let me look at you" Ashley exclaimed. "When are you due?"

"In a couple of months" Aniyah answered.

"Time flies, huh?"

"Don't I know it?" Aniyah replied.

"Well, get your stuff and let's go. We're running late" Ashley joked.

Aniyah made her way back up the stairs, but this time without a grudge. As she grabbed her bag, she noticed she was grinning uncontrollably. She had no idea just how much she longed to be with her sister. It was finally happening. The reunion that seemed to take a lifetime was finally happening and Aniyah couldn't be happier.

As they drove to Alicia's house, Aniyah noticed that small talk wasn't as awkward as she thought it would be. And before she knew it, they'd arrived.

"I'm so nervous" Aniyah shared.

"Why?" Ashley inquired. "It's just Alicia and Alexis. You act like we're meeting somebody famous" she teased.

Aniyah understood that it was just her sisters, but still, she had butterflies in her stomach. This was the first time in forever that they were coming together. She hoped Alexis would be able to make it; but even if not, she was going to enjoy this night.

As they walked to the door, they noticed the door was slightly open. Aniyah and Ashley looked at each other, shrugged, and began to enter.

"Alicia, we're here" they hollered simultaneously.

"Come on to the back" she replied.

Ashley began going through the house as if she'd been there before.

"She has a beautiful home" Aniyah said.

Ashley had to remind herself that her little sister had never visited.

"Yeah, you'll find her house to be quite relaxing" she stated.

"Oh, you've been here before?" Aniyah asked.

"Sure, and now so have you" Ashley joked trying to keep her sister in a good mood.

"It's fine. I'm not taking it personally. I'm simply glad to be here now".

Ashley was impressed with her sister's maturity.

They finally made it to the back and Aniyah broke down.

"Surprise" her sisters yelled.

She was indeed surprised. Not only was Alexis there, but they had decorated the room for a baby shower. Her tears flowed freely.

"I can't believe you guys did this for me" she said grabbing the tissues Alicia handed her.

"Well, we figured, why not? After I told the girls about our conversation and how you genuinely wanted us to get back together, everyone was moved" Alicia explained.

"And when you cancelled your shower just so you could console me, I knew we had to do something" added Alexis. "So we decided to do something nice for you!"

Aniyah was so happy she could do nothing but cry. She was totally speechless. Never in a million years would she have expected something like this.

"You guys are terrific" Aniyah finally managed to say.

"Look, let's get in our pajamas so we can officially begin this baby shower sleepover" Alicia ordered.

"Absolutely" the other sisters said in unison.

While they were changing

clothes, Aniyah found Alexis and decided to take a moment to talk to her.

"How are you doing, Alexis?"

"I'm good. Taking it one day at a time".

"I'm so sorry for your pain, Alexis. I feel so bad. Are you sure you're up to celebrating? It's totally fine if you're not. I'm just glad you're here" Aniyah said.

"You know when you first told me about everything regarding the baby shower, I was still dealing with my loss and it was hard to hear anything else. And I'm truly sorry for being so short with you. I was just still trying to figure out how to handle it."

"You don't have to apologize, Alexis. And we don't have to talk about it if you don't want to. I just want you to know that I'm here for you if ever, whenever you need me".

"Thanks, Aniyah. I really appreciate that. I've missed you so much. I can't believe how long it's been..."

"Well, you know what? We're together now and that's all that matters."

The two sisters were hugging when Alicia and Ashley entered the room.

"What's with the hug fest?" Ashley joked. "I wasn't saying that for you to stop, I want in on it" she continued.

"Me too" Alicia stated.

The sisters noticed they couldn't get too close to Aniyah because her stomach was in the way. Ashley was the first to speak up.

"Aniyah, do you know what you're having?"

"Nah, we decided to wait until the baby is born to find out".

"Well, do you have any names picked out?" Alicia asked.

"If it's a boy, we're going to name him after Justin. And if it's a girl, we're going to name her after Mom".

"That's awesome" Alexis said. "I'm so happy for you, Aniyah".

"I'm happy for us" Aniyah said. "You guys have no idea how long I prayed for this. I mean, I used to pray every night, 'Love Me...Please'. I just wanted you all to love me. I so desired a relationship with my sisters - to be accepted by you. But what's funny is that while I was waiting for that to happen, I started to learn more about myself.

I noticed how lost I originally felt once Mom died because I was so used to having her there telling me what to do. But over time, I began to find my own voice. I began to understand more about my journey and what I was purposed to do. I began to love myself. And it seemed like as soon as I did that everything else just came together".

"It seems like you finally got what Mom was trying to tell you" Ashley said. "I remember having to learn that lesson myself. You can't truly love anyone else until you first love yourself".

"Ain't it the truth?" Alicia responded.

The sisters looked at each

other and laughed.

"Now let's get this party started" Alexis said.

As they headed for the kitchen, Aniyah looked toward the ceiling and simply said, "Thanks, Mom".

Barbara

Barbara and Charles decided that they wanted to celebrate their new beginning with a vow renewal ceremony. In the twenty plus years they'd been married, they'd never had one; in fact, they'd never even had a honeymoon.

When they first got married, they couldn't afford it. Then they had their children and they just got caught up with life. They were so busy being busy that the years simply seemed to escape them.

So when Charles suggested the renewal, Barbara decided to ask about a honeymoon. She was so excited when Charles quickly agreed to her proposal. Now, all they had to do was figure out the details.

"Charles, what were you thinking for the ceremony? Did you want to do something extravagant to include all of our friends and family? Or were you thinking something a bit more intimate?"

He was taken aback that his wife asked for his opinion. Normally, when it came to planning, she automatically took the lead.

"Well, since you asked" Charles started, "I was thinking it best to do something small. Maybe we could just tell the kids about it and let them witness the occasion. Lord knows we gave them plenty of negative things to observe over years - I think they would love to be part of it. To know that their parents have found that happy place again."

Barbara was totally shocked. Her husband never wanted to be involved with planning in the past; never even provided any feedback on the ideas she'd present. And now, not only was he actively engaged, but she loved his thought pattern.

"I think that's an awesome idea, sweetheart."

"Really?" Charles asked surprised.

"Yes, actully it's exactly what I

was thinking. I believe we kinda owe it to the kids. I know it probably wasn't easy for them either. Because although we rarely argued in front of them, I'm sure they felt the tension. They knew something was wrong - even if they didn't know what!"

Charles and Barbara began planning the details for their joyous occasion.

Then Barbara looked at her husband and asked, "When do you think would be a good time to do it, Charles?"

"The sooner the better as far as I'm concerned" he replied.

"But don't we have some other

obligations we've committed to?" she questioned.

"You know what? We very well may, but a wise woman once said, 'Sometimes you have to learn to prioritize'" and offered his wife a wink.

Through the years, Barbara was always pleading with Charles about spending time together and making more of an effort to with her and the children. And though it may have taken a while to sink in, it was comforting to know that he'd heeded her words.

"So, within the next few months?" Barbara inquired.

"I was actually thinking the

next few weeks. It's close to spring break and the kids are normally home during that time, so we can just call to make sure they don't have any other plans" Charles explained.

"But what about you job, sweetheart?" Barbara asked.

"What about it? It'll be here when we get back," he assured. "I have plenty of vacation time stored up so it's not an issue. I'll request the time off as soon as I get to work Monday morning".

Barbara couldn't believe how assertive and aggressive her husband was being. She knew that he possessed those traits, as they were part of the reason she fell in love with him; he just rarely exhibited them toward her.

She contacted her children to tell them the exciting news. They were all so enthused. She let them know that it was going to be just the five of them plus the minister who would perform the ceremony. Barbara didn't know who was more thrilled - her, Charles or the kids.

At this point, she simply needed to determine what she was going to wear. She never really was the type to be caught up with fashion; for her, the ceremony was the focus. Just knowing that she and her husband were finally with one accord delighted her.

It had been such a long time since they both desired the same thing at the same time. And the fact that renewing their vows and reigniting heir marriage was the reason for that bond was incredible.

The day had finally arrived. The children were home and everyone was in a great mood. It reminded Barbara of the good old days. For the first few years of their marriage, she and Charles connected well. They knew each other, and had figured out an effective way of relying on their strengths. And now it seemed they'd found that rhythm again.

The Tates' decided it best to drive in two separate vehicles because they planned to send the children *home after the ceremony. They were going to celebrate with a honeymoon - Charles just refused to tell Barbara where they were headed.*

When she asked to get a sense of what to pack, he responded, "Don't worry about taking anything. You can buy something to wear when we get there".

He wouldn't tell her how long to prepare for the trip; he gave her no clues whatsoever. All he told her was, "Trust me, you're going to love it!"

When they arrived at the church, Barbara found the washroom so she could change her clothes. She decided on a simple white sheath dress with specks of gold sprinkled throughout, along with gold shoes and accessories. Her hair was already in an up-do; so the chosen earrings were a perfect touch.

She was so excited. She felt like she did when she first got married. She was extremely anxious to walk down the aisle to her husband. They'd experienced a great deal, but she was glad they were able to make this journey together.

Barbara heard the music and knew it was time to make her entrance. She hadn't told any of them what she was wearing, so when they saw her, all of their eyes began to swell with tears - especially Charles. Sure, he thought his wife was beautiful, but today she looked *particularly stunning.*

His tears dropped in sync with her footsteps. He couldn't believe this moment in time was finally here. Seeing her like that reminded him why he'd fallen in love with her in the first place. He hated that he'd spent so much time dwelling on the past, but vowed to her that he'd spend the rest of his time actively loving and cherishing her. Treating everyday as though it was the last. Never living with regret.

Barbara sobbed as he spoke his words. She loved her husband's sentiments. It was now her turn to say her vows.

"Charles, I love you so much. It

took a lot of twists and turns for us to wind up on this road, but I'm so glad we're here. We'd been together for so long that at a point, I'd forgotten who I was - I lost focus of myself. I felt lost. That morning when I found you praying, it really moved me.

What I didn't tell you was that for the longest time, I too had been praying. I would pray, 'Love Me...Please'. I thought it was a plea for you to love me. But Charles, what I discovered was that it was really a plea to myself.

I stopped loving myself, which made it easy for me to stop loving those around me - to stop loving life period. I made some bad decisions along the way, but you were there to make sure I didn't fall...even if it meant that you got stepped on in the process.

It was in that time I learned how critical it was for me to love me because until I did that, I wouldn't be able to truly love you the way you needed me to love you. As much as you may have gotten hurt along the way, you always had us in the forefront of your mind.

Despite the pain we may have caused one another, we never gave up hope that one day we'd make it back to this point. I just want you to know that I will be eternally grateful for your unconditional love and I will love you now and forever.

With that, Charles was instructed to kiss his bride - and he did it gladly and with an intensity that resurrected feelings Barbara forgot existed. Their children looked on with such pride and joy. They were truly happy for their parents.

"Mom, Dad, where are you guys going?" They all asked simultaneously.

Barbara looked at her husband awaiting the answer.

"Well, as long as I've known your mother" Charles began "she's always wanted to go to Paris. And I figured what better way to celebrate our renewed love than by going to the City of Love".

Barbara

Barbara stared at Charles with astonishment and a longing gaze.

Once he caught her eyes, she asked, "When we get there, will you Love Me...Please?"

He simply replied, "Absolutely!"